THE
THREE BEARS

ALSO BY W. BRUCE CAMERON

W. BRUCE CAMERON

LILY
TO THE rescue

THE
THREE BEARS

Illustrations by
JAMES BERNARDIN

A TOM DOHERTY ASSOCIATES BOOK

NEW YORK

LILY TO THE RESCUE: THE THREE BEARS

A Starscape Book
Published by Tom Doherty Associates
120 Broadway
New York, NY 10271

www.tor-forge.com

The Library of Congress Cataloging-in-Publication Data is available upon request.

ISBN 978-1-250-76251-1 (trade paperback)
ISBN 978-1-250-76249-8 (hardcover)
ISBN 978-1-250-76250-4 (ebook)

Our books may be purchased in bulk for promotional, educational, or business use. Please contact your local bookseller or the Macmillan Corporate and Premium Sales Department at 1-800-221-7945, extension 5442, or by email at MacmillanSpecialMarkets@macmillan.com.

First Edition: 2022

Printed in the United States of America

0 9 8 7 6 5 4 3 2 1

Dedicated to the wonderful people making lives better at Rosie Animal Adoption in Kirkland, Quebec, Canada.

THE
THREE BEARS

.

1

Everyone knows that Maggie Rose is my girl, and I am her dog. Even squirrels know, because they see me coming at the end of my leash, and they scamper quickly up a tree and then stare down at me.

I always let those squirrels know with a stern look that I could have caught them if I had wanted to, but when I am walking with my girl I need to be careful not to lunge forward because it might pull her over, which I would never do, except for the few times it's happened.

I was with my girl, ignoring a squirrel scolding me from a branch. (A squirrel has no business chattering at a dog, but sometimes they are very rude.) We were crossing the big field that separates Home from Work. Home is where we all sleep and, most importantly, eat. Work is where Mom spends most of her time taking care of animals.

When we are at Work, my girl and I take care of animals, too, mainly by playing with them.

"You get to see Freddy today, Lily!" Maggie Rose sang to me. I wagged because she was happy and because I recognized the name "Freddy." Freddy is a sleek ferret who sometimes sits in a cage at Work. Freddy is my best ferret friend. Actually, I don't know any other ferrets, but if I did, Freddy would be my favorite.

I was still wagging when we walked in the door at Work. Instantly I could smell that Maggie Rose's two brothers were already here, along with Brewster.

Brewster is a dog who lives with us and sleeps on Bryan's bed. He was napping on a dog blanket near the door and raised his head as we came in. I gave him a polite sniff.

"Hey, Maggie Rose," Craig said. He was lugging a heavy bag that smelled of wonderful dog food. "Bryan's outside in the back, playing with two puppies we just rescued."

"Puppies!" Maggie Rose said.

Craig nodded. "I'm almost done stacking dog food, and then I'll come out, too."

My girl ran to the back door and I dashed after her. I didn't know what we were doing, but I was excited to be doing it. It seemed that we were not going into the room of cages where Freddy was waiting for me. That was too bad. But whatever we were doing must be more important.

It wasn't important enough to wake Brewster from his nap, though. Almost nothing can do that.

We burst out into the sunshine and I smelled Bryan and two puppies.

"So cute!" Maggie Rose exclaimed.

One puppy was covered with shaggy dark fur, and one was white with big dark spots. Of course, they were impressed and amazed to see a good dog and her girl.

They ran to me, tripping over themselves. I let them jump on me and chew at my face until Shaggy bit down too hard. Then I flipped him over on his back.

It's the job of older dogs to teach younger dogs how to play properly.

"I've named them Biker and Slam," Bryan told my girl.

Maggie Rose sat on the lawn and the puppies broke away from me and climbed into her lap. She giggled and picked up the spotted one, kissing him on the nose. I trotted over and shoved my face into my girl's face for my own kiss.

Craig came out the back door. There was still no sign of Brewster.

"Those are the worst names ever, Bryan," Maggie Rose told him.

"What are?" Craig asked, falling to his knees and reaching out to the shaggy puppy. Shaggy began chewing Craig's fingers.

"Slime and Blinker," Maggie Rose answered.

Craig hooted.

"That's not what I said!" Bryan responded. "Biker and Slam."

"What? Are you crazy?" Craig answered. "Slacker and Bam?"

"I'm not talking to either of you," Bryan muttered. I saw he was trying not to grin.

I looked up and wagged as Mom came out to see us. She smells different every day. Today she carried the odor of cats.

Craig rose to his feet. "What's wrong, Mom?"

"Your dad just called," Mom said. "He's on his way here with an injured bear. Maggie Rose, can you bring the puppies inside and put them in a kennel? I have to prepare for surgery."

Maggie Rose and Bryan stood and the puppies stared up at them, amazed at how tall the people were. "What happened to the bear?" my girl asked.

"A poacher shot it," Mom replied.

"*What?*" Maggie Rose gasped.

I looked at my girl, sensing her alarm.

"Your dad tracked it down and used a dart

gun to put it into a deep sleep," Mom said. "We'll know more when he gets here."

I followed the humans back into the building. My girl was carrying a puppy in each hand. "What's a poacher?" she asked.

"Somebody who hunts illegally," Craig told her.

"Bet you Dad arrested him," Bryan said.

"Will the bear be okay?" my girl asked. She sounded worried.

"I won't know until I have a chance to examine it," Mom replied.

The two puppies stared at each other. I could tell they were astonished to be so far above the ground. My girl put them in a kennel. They gazed at me, confused. Why were they in there, when I was not?

I followed my nose to where Freddy lurked in a cage. He came to the bars and poked

his snout out to sniff me, and I wagged and sniffed back.

"Come on, Lily!" Maggie Rose told me, turning away.

I had hoped Freddy would be allowed to come out. My girl had let him out once and we'd had a marvelous game of Chase. But it's never happened again.

It didn't happen this time, either. My girl had other plans. People get to decide which animals are allowed to play and which have to remain inside the kennels.

The puppies were back to wrestling in their own cage. That's just how puppies are.

"Lily!" my girl called again. She was standing in an open doorway. "The bear's here. Hurry!"

2

My girl was tense. I thought she must be expecting something exciting to happen. She pulled me over to a bench and sat down with Bryan and Craig. Brewster had already moved his nap to this new location.

I watched, bewildered, as Dad and a woman dressed like Dad trundled a rolling bed into the front room at Work. Lying on that bed, sound asleep, was the biggest, furriest, *smelliest* creature I had ever seen. I did not know how the large animal managed to sleep while being pushed around like that. I was amazed that its own stink didn't wake it up!

"Whoa!" Bryan said. "It's huge!"

Dad and his helper rolled the bed right out of the room again, through a different door. The kids rose to their feet, so I did, too. All Brewster did was open one eye for a moment.

"Here, Maggie Rose," Craig said. He reached down and picked her up in his arms. A moment later Bryan did the same with me, as if my girl and I were a couple of puppies.

At Work there's a room that smells like chemicals, and because Craig and his brother were holding us up high, we could see through a window into that room. Mom was wearing gloves and paper over her mouth. Dad and his friend wheeled the huge animal past the window, and the thing still didn't open its eyes!

Brewster is an expert at napping, but even he would wake up if he were wheeled on a rolling bed into a smelly room.

After a few moments, Dad and his friend came back into the room where we were waiting. His friend left out the front door, but Dad stayed. Bryan and Craig put Maggie Rose and me on the floor and I sniffed Dad curiously. He smelled like trees and dirt and also the napping creature he had just taken for a car ride in a bed.

"Hi, boys; Maggie Rose. Hi, Lily," Dad said. He put his hand down so I could get a better whiff of the creature's smell. I licked his palm and was not particularly happy with the taste.

"Will the bear be okay, Dad?" Maggie Rose asked.

Dad nodded. "I think so. Your mom agrees it's a shallow wound. The bullet just grazed the bear's shoulder."

"Will the poacher go to jail?" Craig wanted to know.

Dad shrugged. "That's up to the judge. All we can do is put the cuffs on them."

"It's so cool you get to arrest people!" Bryan said.

Craig looked at his brother. "We keep hoping he'll arrest *you*."

"You smell, Dad," my girl said, wrinkling her nose.

Dad grinned. "Some bears have a pretty strong odor. That's so if you ever go into a cave and you smell a bear, you'll know to turn right around and run out."

My girl stared at him. "Really?"

Dad laughed. "Well, I doubt that's the reason, but it's something good to keep in mind."

"I'd make Craig go into the cave to check for the bear," Bryan said.

"Like you could make me do anything." Craig snorted.

"When will we find out if the bear is okay?" my girl wanted to know.

Dad held up his hand and looked at it. "Probably at least an hour," he answered. "Your mom said I should tell you to clean out the cat cages."

Bryan groaned.

"Come on, Lily, let's go see kitties," my girl said.

We walked down the back hall to where all the cats lived. Brewster eased to his feet and padded after us.

Soon my girl was moving armfuls of cats from one cage to another. The boys swept out cages and squirted a stinky liquid into each. Brewster decided this was more than he could take and circled up for a snooze. I joined him. I like cats, but not if all they are going to do is sit in their cages and stare at me.

Brewster moved over to make room for me. I might not be as good at sleeping as the huge stinky creature, but I'm not bad, either. Napping is one of my main skills.

A short time later, the door to the hallway opened. I was instantly awake.

"Kids, can you come out here, please?" Mom said.

There was something very tense in the way the children glanced at each other. Silently, they followed Mom out into the front room.

Our nails clicking, Brewster and I brought up the rear. We could smell that Mom had gotten some of the stinky creature's odors on her clothing.

"What's wrong, Mom?" my girl asked. "Did something bad happen with the bear?"

"Where's Dad?" Craig wanted to know.

Mom pursed her lips. "The bear's fine. I cleaned the wound and stitched it up. But when I examined her, I realized that she's got cubs. She gave birth this winter. I can't tell how many, but she's had at least one. Your dad left to change his uniform and go back up into the mountains."

"Babies?" Maggie Rose replied. I nosed her hand because she seemed worried, and needed to know she had a good dog by her side.

"How come Dad didn't see the cubs when he found the bear?" Bryan asked.

Mom shrugged. "They might have been hiding. Dad didn't know to look for them, but he knows now, and he's getting some people from his department to try to find them. Hopefully before nightfall."

Craig stood up straight. "I'd like to help search."

"Me, too," Bryan said.

"And me," my girl added.

Mom gazed at us thoughtfully.

3

Whatever they were talking about was too much for Brewster. He collapsed on the floor with his eyes closed.

"Your dad and I discussed it," Mom said. "We knew you'd all want to help. But when we get there, you must do exactly as your dad and I say. Is that understood?"

I felt the children brighten. "Lily can help, too!" my girl exclaimed. "Once we find the cubs, she can calm them down. They'll be so scared without their mom."

Bryan said. "And I've got Brewster. He's part hound dog. He'll track them."

At his name we all looked at Brewster, who was making soft snoring noises.

"Good luck with that," Craig said.

"I need to wait here for the people from the zoo to come pick up the bear," Mom said. "She, and hopefully her cubs, will stay with them until she's recovered, and then your dad will release them all into the mountains. Meanwhile, you should go home and get ready. Put on your hiking boots, and slip jackets into your backpacks—Echo Lake is over ten thousand feet above sea level. It's a lot cooler up there."

Brewster and I leaped to our feet when the children hurried out the front door. I dutifully kept the leash slack between Maggie

Rose and me, but Brewster found many things to sniff along the way. Some of them were spots that needed to be peed on. "Come on, Brewster," Bryan kept saying, tugging him along.

Clearly we were headed across the field to Home. It was the most fun we'd had all day, except when we'd crossed the same field to go to Work.

Once we were Home, Craig and Bryan and Maggie Rose hurried from room to room. Brewster and I decided to stay in the living room. Mom normally doesn't like us to sleep on the couch, but we could feel that everyone was excited, so it seemed like a special occasion. We climbed up and settled down in comfort.

"I can't find my hiking boots!" Bryan called from his room.

"Wear Maggie Rose's ballet slippers," Craig answered.

When we heard Mom's car in the driveway, Brewster and I both eased down off the couch. We are smart dogs.

But we didn't have to be smart this time, because Mom didn't even walk in the door. Instead, Maggie Rose called, "Mom's here!" and we all ran out and jumped in her car.

Now I understood why everyone had been so excited. We were going for a car ride! Even Brewster was alert and wagging. He helped me keep an eye out the window for squirrels and other situations that would need some barking.

"I'll bet you the cubs are lonesome without their mommy," my girl said.

"Not just lonesome," Mom said from up front. "Bear cubs can't fend for themselves. They need the mother bear to find food for them, and to protect them from predators. There are all sorts of threats to baby bears. Coyotes, mountain lions—even other bears."

"Then we need to find them!" Maggie Rose said, a flicker of worry in her voice.

Out the window I saw a dog walking with a man. I barked, though Brewster did not. "Lily, no!" my girl scolded.

Why was she cross with me when Brewster was the one who forgot to bark?

In fact, Brewster had decided to lie down and drool a little on Bryan's shorts. He doesn't understand about car-riding behavior. He should have watched me—I would

have shown him what to do. Instead, he fell asleep.

Because he was sleeping, Brewster didn't notice the change in the air as the clean, cool smell of Up in the Mountains came wafting into the car. Up in the Mountains is a place like Work or Home. It has fewer people, more animals, and much of the time lots of snow. I wagged because I had always had fun with my girl when we went to Up in the Mountains.

Brewster roused himself when we swung into a flat dirt area with several cars parked nearby. It was a parking lot. It's a strange thing, but people take car rides to parking lots all the time, even though when you get there, there's not much to do.

When my girl opened the door I bounded out and shook, wagging because I smelled Dad. Brewster immediately trotted to the end of his leash, found a big rock, sniffed it several times, and then turned and lifted his leg against it. Apparently, that's why Brewster thought we had driven all this way: so he could pee on a rock.

"There's Echo Lake!" Maggie Rose said, pointing. "So pretty!"

"And there's Dad," Craig added.

"James! We're here. James!" Mom called, waving. Sometimes she calls Dad that. I don't know why she can't learn his name, but it doesn't seem to worry Dad, so I don't let it bother me.

Dad was talking with some other grown-ups, though he waved at us when Mom called the wrong name. We all strolled over to meet him, stopping here and there because there were a couple of big rocks that Brewster wanted to make part of his territory.

Dad broke from the cluster of people and came over to meet us.

"Good timing," Dad said, smiling. "We're

just getting started. We're going to begin where we caught up with the mother bear and fan out from there in groups of three."

"I can lead our group," Craig said. He stood a little taller, holding still like a dog who wants to show that he's ready to play as long as the other dogs understand who's in charge. "Me and Bryan and Maggie Rose make three."

"No way." Bryan scowled. "Who says you get to be the leader?"

"My survival course badge, that's who," Craig said back.

Dad sighed. "Boys. Cut it out. We all need to cooperate. I'm going to ask you kids to search in *a very important area*. Okay?"

Everyone nodded solemnly. I glanced at Brewster, and even he seemed to nod. Apparently, we all knew that something serious was happening.

4

I need the three of you . . ." Dad paused. "to take the path all the way around Echo Lake."

There was a short silence.

"What? We've hiked that a million times. We're not going to find the bear cubs *there*," Bryan blurted.

"We'd be a lot more help off the trails, like everybody else," Craig said.

Dad crossed his arms. "This is interesting. Every other team is going where I've told them to go, and none of them are arguing."

"Maybe you should just do what your father asks," Mom put in.

Everyone was quiet for a moment. "Yes, sir," Craig finally muttered.

"Have you had lunch?" Dad asked.

"There wasn't time," Mom told him.

"All right," Dad said. "I'll give you some money. Go get some sandwiches and bottles of water up at the lodge. You can take them with you, make a picnic out of it."

"Thank you, Dad," Maggie Rose said. I was watching Brewster. He was sniffing around. It was clear that he wanted to lie down for a nap, but his only choices were dusty ground or sharp gravel. He wasn't too happy.

"I'll hold on to the dogs. You kids go get your food," Mom said. My girl handed my leash to Mom, and the two boys ran off toward a very big house not far away.

Maggie Rose did not go with them. She stayed behind with Mom and Dad. Brewster also stayed with us. Mom had his leash as well.

"I'm glad you're here, Maggie Rose. You're my game warden girl," Dad said. "Okay, I'm heading out, Chelsea. I'll see you soon."

"Good luck," Mom told him.

Dad walked away, following Craig and Bryan. "Boys! Hold up!"

Bryan and Craig waited while Dad went to them. They talked a little, and then Dad headed off to talk to some more grown-ups. I saw Bryan and Craig enter the big house.

Now it was just two dogs and two people out here in the parking lot. What were we doing? Were we waiting for something fun to happen?

Mom smiled down at Maggie Rose. "What is it, honey?"

"Couldn't I go with you instead?" my girl asked.

"You heard your dad. He wants groups of three. Why don't you want to go with your brothers?"

"It's just that they argue all the time. They're not nice to each other," Maggie Rose complained.

"I'll walk you over to the lodge. Come on," Mom told her. We headed slowly in the direction Bryan and Craig had taken. "Well, your brothers like to insult each other as a way of saying they love each other. Don't take it seriously."

Maggie Rose sighed. "Okay."

Mom paused at the wooden steps of the big building. "Tell you what, though. I'll say something to them about it. And if it bothers you, you should say something, too. Never feel as if you can't share your feelings."

Brewster lifted his nose. He'd noticed the food smells coming from inside.

"Okay, Mom. Aren't you going to look for the bears, too?"

"I'll partner up with a couple of the rangers. I can't stay too long. I'll call Craig on his cell phone when it's time for us all to leave."

"But Mom!" Maggie Rose sounded alarmed. "What if we haven't found the cubs before you have to go?"

"Hon, there are a lot of people here to look for the cubs," Mom said.

"But we want to stay until they're found," Maggie Rose insisted. "Mom, please, can't we ride home with Dad, instead?"

Mom looked down at Maggie Rose and seemed to be thinking. "Well, okay," she said at last. "Make sure you tell your dad. All three of you kids will ride home with him."

I watched in confusion as Maggie Rose

climbed up the steps to the big house. Mom stayed behind, still holding my leash.

Brewster was anxious because he had lost sight of Bryan. I could tell, even though he didn't really act like it. Brewster doesn't act like he's worked up about much of anything.

Soon Bryan and Craig hurried out of the big doors and down the steps.

"Did you see your sister?" Mom asked.

Craig nodded. "I gave her some money. She'll be out soon."

"Maggie Rose told me something," Mom replied. "She said she's uncomfortable with the way you tease each other. I told her you don't mean it, but maybe you could ease up a little? To tell you the truth, it sometimes gets on my nerves, too."

Bryan and Craig looked at each other. "I'll let up if the idiot does," Bryan said.

"I'll ignore when he's being a jerk," Craig agreed.

"I'm glad we've come to this understanding," Mom said wryly. "All right, as soon as your sister comes out, you can get going. And remember what your dad said—stay on the path around the lake! That's your assignment."

Mom left. Brewster went to Bryan and sat and I knew why. Bryan's hands showed that he'd been touching peanut butter not long before. It's one of the best things about Bryan—how often his fingers smell like that.

Maggie Rose came out. "I bought some dog treats, too," she announced happily.

"Let's go find a picnic table. Buying lunch made me hungry!" Bryan declared.

We walked a short way and the kids settled in at a wooden table. Brewster and I, the dogs of the situation, sat with our mouths within easy reach. Crisp paper was unwrapped, flooding the air with wonderful sandwich-type odors.

Soon Brewster and I went on full alert because we could hear chewing up there. There should be chewing down here!

"Okay," Craig said after a long, long time of little talking and no feeding good dogs. "I say we go counter-clockwise. Hike along the road first."

They rose to their feet. Maggie Rose handed me a cheese treat, and Bryan gave Brewster peanut butter!

"Let's go," Bryan said.

5

Brewster and I could both sense the excitement in the children as they led us down to a paved road nearly empty of cars. We began walking along a gravel trail alongside the road. To one side was a hill covered with trees and rocks. To the other, the land was flat. Ahead I could sense the crisp smell of water. I knew there must be a huge pond there.

It was going to be a great walk. Brewster

was happy, too. He celebrated by sniffing and lifting his leg on large stones.

"Let's go uphill," Bryan suggested. "The bears aren't going to be this close to the road."

Brewster had found a particularly amazing scent and was checking it out carefully, so we all halted. The children looked up the gentle slope. "I don't know," Craig told Bryan. "That's not really the trail. We're supposed to stick to the trail."

"But our mission is to find the bears," Bryan said. "And the trees up there are spread out enough. We'll be able to see the lake the whole time."

My girl shook her head. "We should stick to the trail," she said. "Don't you think, Craig?"

"Why is Craig in charge?" Bryan demanded.

"Because I took a survival course," Craig answered.

"See the elk?" my girl asked.

"Fine," Bryan said. "I'll go up there. You guys can stay down here."

"No," Craig said.

"Guys!"

The boys blinked at Maggie Rose. She pointed. "See? What's it doing?"

I had lowered my nose to sniff what Brewster had been sniffing. It *was* interesting! But now I snapped my head up at a new, strong odor. Down the road from us, a large deer creature was striding back and forth at the edge of the pavement.

"It's afraid of the road," Bryan observed.

"That's good. Elks *should* be afraid of the road," Craig said. "Even though there are hardly any cars, you never know when one might come along."

Brewster could smell something else, I could tell, because his gaze had broken away from the huge deer. He was looking up in the trees. When I turned my head in that direction, I couldn't smell anything. But a faint, distressed cry came to my ears.

There was something up there, something scared. Brewster and I both knew it. We sat, looking at our people, waiting for them to know it, too.

"It's acting like it wants to cross the road," my girl said.

"If we keep walking, we're going to scare it even more," Bryan said.

Craig looked at him. "Okay, we'll go up in the trees a little bit, keep out of the elk's way, let it decide what it wants to do."

I figured that the children had heard the tiny, mewling call, because we turned away from the road and began to climb up the hill.

"Hear that? What was that?" Maggie Rose cried.

"I didn't hear anything," Bryan answered.

"There! Hear it?" my girl said.

The soft call came down out of the trees again.

Craig straightened. "Yes!"

"It's the bears!" Bryan exclaimed.

All at once, everyone decided to *run*. My girl and I fell behind Bryan. Craig was out in front.

"Craig!" Maggie Rose called. "Wait for us!"

Craig halted. We all reached him and stopped. Brewster's tongue was lolling out of his mouth.

"You're right, Maggie Rose. We need to stick together," Craig said.

"I see something," Maggie Rose told him. "See? It's moving."

The way Brewster's nose twitched told me that he could smell what I could smell. Another creature was close by, one that carried pretty much the same odor as the giant deer we had seen by the road.

"Yes!" Bryan said. "I see it!"

I caught a flicker of movement. A much smaller deer raised its head and bawled at the sky.

"It's a baby!" my girl said. "Why is it crying?"

Craig turned and looked back the way we'd come. "Its mother is on the other side of the road. They got separated."

"Can we help?" my girl wanted to know.

Craig was silent.

"Maybe we should call Dad?" Bryan asked.

Craig nodded slowly. "We could do that. But he's busy leading the search for the bear cubs."

"The elk was by the side of the road because her baby crossed over here," Maggie Rose said. "But the mother's afraid to walk on the pavement."

"You know what we could do?" Craig said. "We could head up the hill and come back around the calf from behind. Sort of shoo it back toward the road. Once it sees its mother, it'll run to her."

"Let's do it!" Bryan said.

I could still see the little deer. I hoped we'd go up closer so that everyone could smell it. But instead we struck off in a slightly different direction.

Brewster glanced at me. I decided to trot confidently at my girl's side so that he would think I knew what we were doing.

The small deer had stopped bawling and was watching us with dark eyes, not moving.

"What if we can't scare it?" Maggie Rose asked.

With a toss of its head, the deer wheeled around and headed deeper into the woods. The children watched it go, their shoulders slumping.

"I don't think we need to worry about not scaring it," Craig said.

"It's going in the wrong direction." Maggie Rose sounded worried.

"We were too close," Craig told her.

"So let's go up even farther, so that we're for sure behind it," Bryan said. "Circle around from like fifty yards away."

Craig nodded. "We could do that. But we've kind of forgotten about the bears."

"The bears could be around *here*," Bryan told him. "We can search and help the elk calf at the same time."

Craig looked at Maggie Rose.

"I think we should help the baby elk get back to its mommy," my girl said softly.

6

The children led us farther into the woods. I could tell we were all about to do something important.

The slope flattened out, making the going easier for Brewster. He wanted to mark most of the big stones and logs we passed, but Bryan didn't slow down to let him. Brewster would sort of raise his leg and wave it past a tree and keep going, pulled forward by Bryan's hand on his leash.

I could still smell the small deer.

"Where did the baby elk go?" Maggie Rose asked, peering into the trees.

"I see it. Look, close to that rock? It's moving," Craig told her, pointing.

"It's moving the *wrong way*," Bryan said.

"Poor little thing." My girl sounded sad.

Suddenly, Brewster wasn't interested in sniffing along the tree roots anymore. He stood stiffly, staring back behind us into the thick woods, nose lifted. Could he smell something special? I sniffed the air, but I just got the usual scents of Up in the Mountains.

"Come on, Brewster," Bryan told him. "We need to keep going."

Brewster knew what Bryan wanted and went along, following the leash. But after a few steps he twisted to look back.

"Brewster smells something," Bryan said.

"The bears?" Maggie Rose asked.

"I don't know," Bryan answered.

Now that we were all standing still, the faint breeze ruffled the tree branches and I suddenly understood what Brewster had noticed. There was a dog-smell on the air, but it wasn't dog. It was dog and not-dog at the same time.

"There are two of them, see?" Craig said softly. I glanced at him because he seemed tense.

"No, see what?" my girl asked him.

"Just to the left of where that tree is leaning over. They aren't moving. Just watch. There!" Craig pointed.

"I saw something," Maggie Rose said.

"Me, too," Bryan said. "What are they?"

Craig gave them a solemn look. "Coyotes. Young ones."

Everyone was quiet for a moment. Brewster still stared hard into the trees, but I was focused on my girl. I knew she and her brothers were worried.

"They're hunting," Craig said.

"They're hunting us?" Maggie Rose gasped. Alarm flashed off of her skin.

Craig shook his head. "No. Two young coyotes wouldn't come after three humans and two dogs. No, it's the elk calf they're after. That's why it's been running away. Somehow the coyotes got between it and its mother, and now we're between it and the coyotes."

"We have to protect the baby!" Maggie Rose said.

"That's what we're doing," Craig told her. "All we have to do is stay between the calf and the coyotes, and it'll be safe."

"Let's do it," Bryan said.

We turned from the not-dogs and began moving briskly on the trail of the small deer, tracking her scent. The humans had decided

that they would rather play with the small deer than the not-dogs.

The deer trotted on thin legs ahead of us. We followed as it kept going deeper and deeper into the woods.

Bryan glanced over his shoulder. "They're still behind us."

Craig looked back as well. "Yes, but not any

closer. They're hanging back because of us, and because of the dogs."

"Good dog, Lily!" Maggie Rose told me.

I straightened a little, happy I was being a good dog. Brewster peered at me, wondering what I was doing that he wasn't.

The going became easier because we were headed downhill. The trees thinned out, and I could easily see the small deer far ahead.

Every so often it would stop moving and peer around. I decided it could smell Brewster and me, but it wasn't yet sure about playing with us. Some animals are like that. They don't understand that playing with dogs is the most fun there is.

Behind us, the two small not-dogs were tracking us, moving from tree to tree, almost as if they were hiding. Brewster was more upset about them than I was. He kept looking back.

Brewster is older than I, and sometimes I

wonder if there have been things in his long life that make him a little careful about other creatures. Maybe that's why he naps all the time—because he's tired from all the things that have happened to him.

I'm not like that. I'm always happy to play with any other animal, until it shows me that it's not a good playmate.

Up ahead, I heard the small deer make a sound. It was unhappy and afraid.

My girl heard it, too. "It's really scared!" she said.

"I don't think it understands that we're trying to help," Craig said. "As far as it's concerned, we're chasing it, just like the coyotes."

We'd gone a long way, past many trees that I knew Brewster wanted to mark. Everyone was focused on the small deer except Brewster. He was still paying attention to the not-dogs behind us.

When Brewster's whole body stiffened, I knew that he had sensed something. I turned my nose backward and realized that the not-dogs had gone away.

"Look at that!" Maggie Rose exclaimed.

Everyone halted.

The air brought with it the odor of the small deer. Its scent had gotten stronger, somehow. I turned my gaze forward and realized that it wasn't just one small deer, now. There were lots of very *large* deer, lurking in the woods. All of them raised their heads as the small deer made a mewling noise and ran to them.

It was a pack of giant deer, and the small deer belonged with them. It was her family!

"And look, there's the mother elk from the side of the road!" Bryan said.

7

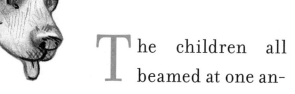

The children all beamed at one another and at the huge deer. One of them smelled familiar. I'd smelled it before, back when we'd first started our walk. This one walked over to the small deer we'd been following and lowered her head to the little one. They touched noses briefly.

A lot of animals see dogs touching noses and decide it's a good idea and start doing it themselves. But they don't usually learn how to sniff butts, which is the best part.

"We rescued a baby elk!" Maggie Rose said, bouncing up and down on her toes a little. "I can't wait to tell Mom."

Craig looked around. "All right, let's get back to the road." He pointed and I followed his finger, curious. I couldn't smell anything interesting in that direction, so why was he pointing that way?

Bryan shook his head. "No. The road's this way, not that way."

Maggie Rose frowned. "Are you sure?"

Craig gazed at her, then raised his head and peered at the sky. "With all these clouds, I can't tell where the sun is."

Brewster sat, yawning, and scratched himself behind the ear. I yawned myself. Brewster can always do that to me: make me yawn, even if I am not in the mood to do so.

"We should follow Brewster," Bryan suggested. "He has a hound dog's nose."

Craig snorted. "Brewster looks like he's ready to take a nap."

"No. Watch. Come on, Brewster!"

Brewster eased to his feet, eyeing Bryan suspiciously.

"Let's go! Find the road! Come on!" Bryan pulled Brewster a few steps. Brewster glanced at me and then went along. The rest of us followed.

"You're *pulling* him," Craig told Bryan. "Let him lead."

"I know how to handle my own dog," Bryan answered.

"Okay, then drop the leash. See where he goes," Craig said.

Bryan dropped Brewster's leash. "Find the road, Brewster!" Bryan told his dog. "Find the road!"

Brewster looked at us. We all looked at him. I figured he was supposed to do some sort of trick and then we would all get treats.

Brewster sat, and Bryan groaned.

"Some hound dog," Craig said. "Let's go." He turned in another direction. Maggie Rose and I got ready to follow.

"No," Bryan said stubbornly. "Who says you get to decide?"

"I'm the oldest, and I'm the only one who's had survival training," Craig answered.

"You're the oldest and the dumbest," Bryan said.

"Yeah? Well you're dumb to infinity."

"You're dumb to infinity times infinity."

"Please!" Maggie Rose cried.

We all stared at her, and I went to lick her hand. My girl was upset. "We're lost and you're just *arguing*!"

Everyone was quiet for a moment. "Okay," Craig finally said. "We know the elk were in front of us. So if we walk away from them, we'll be going back the way we came. All right?"

Bryan shrugged. "Okay," he agreed. But he didn't sound sure. "I still think it'd be faster to just head straight back to the road."

"Thank you, Bryan," Maggie Rose said gratefully.

We took more of a walk. The boys kept checking back behind us. After a short while, Bryan shook his head. "I can't see the elk anymore."

"That's okay," Craig replied. "This part was downhill, remember? And now we're headed back and going uphill. The road's this way."

We trudged along some more. After a little time, we left the area that Brewster had already marked. Now we were exploring a new place, where he was eager to lift his leg.

"Come on, Brewster," Bryan said more than once. There was a gentle note to his voice, though.

His voice wasn't gentle at all when he said to Craig, "Now we're going *down*hill."

Craig paused, frowning. We all waited for him to do something, though I didn't know what. I looked up at Maggie Rose. "Are you sure this is the right way, Craig?" she asked.

Craig shook his head. "No, not completely. Listen." He reached into his backpack and pulled out a phone. "I'll just call Dad."

"He'll be mad at us. We left the trail," Maggie Rose said.

Craig sighed. "Yeah. I know. But I think we have to—oh."

He was looking down at the phone.

"What's wrong?" Maggie Rose asked.

"The battery's dead," Craig said slowly. "We can't call anybody."

"So we're really lost?" my girl asked in a small voice.

"No," Craig answered quickly. "Of course not. Look, we only went, what, maybe forty-five minutes from the road? So it's not that far."

"Then why haven't we found it yet?" Bryan wanted to know.

"Okay," Craig said. "If we climb up to the top of the hill, we should be able to see the lake and the lodge."

"Is that from your survival training?" Bryan asked with a bit of a sneer.

"Do you have a better idea?" Craig demanded.

Everyone struck off in yet another direction. Gradually, the smell of where we'd been that afternoon left the air. We were truly exploring, and it was fun to sniff out new animal odors in the soil and along the trees and bushes.

Craig stopped. "Let's drink some water," he said.

Brewster and I watched as the children searched in their packs, but all they brought out were bottles of water that hardly smelled like anything at all. "Let's give some to the dogs, too," Bryan said.

Maggie Rose cupped her hands and Bryan carefully dribbled some sweet water into them. "Here, Lily," she offered. I carefully licked up the drink, loving my girl, kissing her hands when the water was gone.

"I didn't realize when we got up here that the trees would be so thick," Craig said,

looking around. "We won't be able to see anything."

"So we really are lost." Bryan's voice was flat.

Craig gazed at him and then nodded. "Yeah, we're lost."

There was a long silence. "I'm scared, Craig," Maggie Rose finally said.

8

Sometimes people use words to tell each other things. Sometimes, like dogs, they pass messages without making any sounds.

This seemed to be one of the no-sound times, because the two boys exchanged a long look. Then Craig bent over so he could see my girl's face. "I don't think you should be scared, Maggie Rose. We've got a lot of daylight left. And the road goes for miles.

All we have to do is find it and we'll be able to get back to the lodge."

"Right," Bryan agreed. "Besides, we all knew we weren't going to see the bears right by the lake. There are too many people on the path. Out here, we could find them before anybody else!"

"Sure! We'd be heroes!" Craig said, grinning.

"People would carry Maggie Rose on their shoulders and name an airport after her," Bryan added. He sounded happy. He sounded as if he were *trying* to sound happy.

My girl giggled.

Craig lifted his eyes to the sky. "Still can't see the sun." He studied his wrist. "It's just past three. We should go this way, because . . ." He paused and looked at Bryan. "Well, what direction do you think we should go, Bryan? Maggie Rose?"

"I don't know," my girl answered.

"Why don't we keep going in the direction we've been heading?" Bryan suggested. "Even if it doesn't lead to the road, we might find a trail. And the trail will take us *somewhere*."

"That's a great idea, Bryan," Craig told him.

Whatever they had been talking about seemed to lift their spirits, and that made me cheerful, too. I trotted happily at the end of my leash. We were still exploring new places, it seemed, and Brewster enjoyed leaving his marks over such a large area.

When the strong scent of a new animal reached us, Brewster and I were alert, waiting for the humans to react.

Suddenly Maggie Rose gasped. "Look over there! I see the bear cubs!"

Everyone ran. Up ahead I saw two heavy, dark-colored animals snuffling along the ground. A pair of huge squirrels!

"I see them!" Bryan called.

Even with Maggie Rose and Bryan running behind us, Brewster and I were straining at the end of our leashes. We were making so much noise that the squirrels both stared in alarm. Each was chubby and about the size of a cat.

I knew what was going to happen next. They would scamper up a tree.

I have never caught a squirrel, and I'm not sure what would happen if I did, but I'd really like to find out. I knew for sure I would be able to catch at least one of these big ones before they made it to a branch out of my reach.

"Whoa, hold on, those aren't bears," Craig said. Maggie Rose dragged me to a stop.

I could make no sense of this and looked up at her. Why was she keeping me from catching a big squirrel?

The squirrels ignored the trees and both dove into a hole in the ground. Oh, *those* kind of squirrels! I'd met them before. They're too lazy to climb trees. Instead, they go into holes.

"Marmots," Bryan said disgustedly. "They're just marmots."

"I'm sorry, Bryan," Maggie Rose told him.

I pulled my girl over to the hole so I could stick my nose in and drink up the smell of big fat squirrel. Bright dark eyes glittered back at me.

"I did a report on marmots for school," Bryan said. "Biggest squirrels in the squirrel family."

"I thought *you* were the biggest squirrel in the squirrel family," Craig told him.

"What does that make you, then?" Bryan grinned at him. "You're bigger than I am."

"I'm sorry," Maggie Rose said again.

"No, you know what? Forget about it. I was fooled, too," Bryan replied. "I saw a furry critter and my brain said it was what we're looking for."

They stood for a moment. Brewster nosed the ground, and I knew before he did it that he was going to lie down.

"I guess we'd better keep going," Craig finally said.

Bryan tugged at Brewster's leash, and Brewster got wearily to his feet.

I had no sense of where our people were taking us. I just knew it was deeper and deeper into the woods. Brewster finally had to give up on his project to lift his leg on every tree we passed. There were just too many of them.

After we'd been walking for a long time, I could sense my girl getting tired. It showed in the way her feet dragged just a little, and how her grip on my leash had grown slack. "Craig? I need to stop and rest," she said.

"I think we should keep going," Craig answered.

"But we're lost," Bryan pointed out. "If we keep going, won't that just make us lost-er?"

"I don't think that's a word," Craig told him.

"What should I say?" Bryan asked.

"More lost," Craig advised.

"There. You admit it. We're more lost," Bryan said. He sounded as if he'd won something.

"What time is it?" my girl asked.

Craig lifted his hand and stared at it. "It's a little after five."

"Well, that's good. Dad will start looking for us when we don't show up at the car," Bryan said.

"Dad?" Craig asked. "But we came up here with Mom. He thinks we're going home with Mom. That's what he said when we were walking to the lodge."

Maggie Rose shook her head. "But I . . . I told Mom we'd go home with Dad."

There was a short silence. Brewster eyed the pine needles, getting ready to lie down. Bryan threw up his hands. "Great. Dad thinks we're driving home with Mom, and Mom thinks we're driving home with Dad."

Craig nodded. His whole body seemed to sag. "So nobody's going to realize we're stuck out here until they both get home."

"And that could be after dark," Maggie Rose said.

Brewster collapsed onto his stomach and rolled onto his side. Bryan dropped Brewster's leash. "This is bad," Bryan said.

9

I watched Craig as he looked around. I glanced around, too, but all I saw were trees and trees. "I think," he said slowly, "that we should stop before we get even more lost."

"What do you mean? Stop? Here?" Now my girl was looking around, too. "We can't just stop, Craig. We have to get to the road."

I touched her hand with my nose. Whatever was upsetting her, she was with a good dog who loved her.

"I know," Craig agreed. "But it's not going to be daylight much longer. Before the sun goes down, we need water, food, and shelter. Here is as good a place as any."

Maggie Rose shook her head wildly. "Here is not good! No one will find us here!"

Craig gave Bryan a long look, and Bryan turned to my girl. "Maggie Rose. Listen. Craig's right. We don't know when they'll even start searching for us. We have to prepare for it to get dark."

My girl bit her lip. I nosed her hand again. Brewster, still sprawled on the ground, sighed and shut his eyes.

"What I learned in survival class is, the first rule is, don't panic," Craig said, holding up a finger. Then he held up another. "The second rule is, make a plan."

"So what's the plan?" Bryan asked.

Craig thought about it. "Okay, first, I guess we should check our water supply."

Craig sat down, and the other children did the same. Brewster flapped his tail against the ground.

When the kids took off their backpacks and unzipped them, the sound got Brewster's attention. He raised his head, probably wondering the same thing I was. Dinner?

"Two bottles of water," Maggie Rose said.

"Three," said Bryan.

"I've got three, too. Okay, that's good," Craig said. "We just ate a little while ago, so even though we haven't got any food, it's not so bad. We can last until morning with no food as long as we've got water."

"Actually—" said Bryan. He reached into his own backpack and pulled something out. I recognized the smell and began to wag my tail. Brewster eased to his feet.

"You brought a jar of peanut butter?" Craig asked, laughing softly.

"No," Bryan replied patiently. He reached

into his bag and brought out another jar, and another. Brewster and I were both wagging now. I did my very best Sit to encourage some sharing.

Craig shook his head. "Who brings *three* jars of peanut butter on a hike around Echo Lake?"

Bryan shrugged. "I didn't want to run out."

"Yeah, I guess not."

"Well, if you're complaining, maybe you don't want any," Bryan said. He stuffed the jars of peanut butter back into his back-pack.

"I'm not complaining, Bryan!" Maggie Rose said quickly.

"No, I'm not complaining. You are like, the genius master of peanut butter, Bryan," Craig said. "So okay! We've got water, and thanks to Professor Peanut Butter, food. We won't starve or die of thirst. The only thing we have to worry about now is temperature. Once the sun's all the way down, it's going to get chilly pretty fast this high up in the mountains. We need some shelter."

Bryan looked around. "Here? What do you mean?"

"We'll have to put one together with what we have," Craig told him.

"I don't think I have anything to make a shelter from," Maggie Rose said slowly.

"Well," Bryan said to Craig, "you did promise to build Maggie Rose an airport."

Everyone laughed, which made my girl relax a little.

Craig picked up a very long branch from the ground. "We can build a lean-to."

Maggie Rose brightened. "I know what that is! We find a tree limb close to the ground and lean branches up against it."

"Branches with leaves or pine needles," Bryan added.

"See? You know what to do," Craig said.

Bryan unclipped Brewster's leash, and my girl unsnapped mine. Then we played with sticks!

Everyone seemed to have forgotten how to throw them, though. Craig and Maggie Rose and Bryan found big sticks, most of them covered with dead pine needles, and dragged them over near where Brewster had decided to take a nap. I ran after my girl and grabbed her sticks with my teeth and tried to play Tug-a-Stick. This is, of course, the right thing to do with sticks if nobody's throwing them.

"No, Lily," my girl told me. I found this baffling. Why would anyone say "no" about a stick?

When they decided they didn't want to play anymore, I saw that all the sticks were leaning up against a low tree branch in a shape that reminded me a little of a doghouse.

"I still think an airport would have been a better idea," Bryan said. "We could have flown home on an airplane."

"It doesn't look very warm," Maggie Rose said softly. "The ground is going to be cold."

They were silent for a moment. Craig squinted at the sky. "Sun's going down. That's why it's getting chilly." He looked at my girl. "You're right. The lean-to will keep some of our heat in, but it's going to be a pretty cold night. I'm not sure what choice we have, though."

Maggie Rose crouched and peered into the not-doghouse. "I have an idea," she said.

10

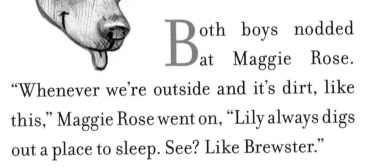

Both boys nodded at Maggie Rose. "Whenever we're outside and it's dirt, like this," Maggie Rose went on, "Lily always digs out a place to sleep. See? Like Brewster."

When my girl said my name, the boys looked at me. Now that she had said Brewster's name, they were all looking at him.

Brewster was lying in the hollow he had scraped out for himself while I was busy helping with sticks. As if he could tell that we were gazing at him, he opened one eye.

"The hole helps keep him warm," Maggie Rose said. "It's like a dog bed. We could do that. We could scoop out a dog bed and fill it up with pine needles. That would be warmer than the dirt. Softer, too."

"Hey." Craig was smiling. "That's a really good idea, Maggie Rose."

After that, Bryan and Craig crawled in underneath the sticks and began digging out soil with their hands.

"I'll give Lily and Brewster treats," Maggie Rose said.

Naturally Brewster snapped open his eyes at that word. We did very beautiful Sits for my girl, who handed out delicious, meaty treats from her bag. As I gently took the wonderful snacks from her fingers, I noticed that Brewster was getting as much as

I was, even though I had done all the work with the sticks while he'd slept.

That was unfair. I didn't hold it against Maggie Rose, though. People sometimes don't notice when one dog is being much better than another. But I loved my girl all the same.

Bryan and Craig finished playing with dirt and began carrying handfuls of dry, smelly pine needles into the hole they'd made. When they were finished, they stood back and looked at what they'd done. They seemed proud.

I thought that what Maggie Rose had done was much more important. The boys had just dug in the dirt. Anybody could do that. Maggie Rose, on the other hand, had handed out a lot of dog treats. Now, *that* was something to be proud of.

Bryan looked around. "Getting colder by the minute," he said. "Not sure lying in there is really going to be warm."

"You're right," Craig said glumly. "Even though it's summer, this high up, we could get too cold. It's called hypothermia. Our bodies need to keep a certain temperature or we could freeze to death, even though it's not freezing out."

"Wait! I know!" Maggie Rose said.

We all looked at her. Her bright voice suggested to me that she had thought of where she could find more dog treats. "We'll cuddle with the dogs," she told her brothers. "You and Bryan lie on each side of Brewster, because he's bigger. And I'll hug Lily. Even on cold nights, she puts out heat like a furnace."

Craig nodded and smiled. "Excellent, Maggie Rose."

Bryan clapped his hands. "How about some peanut butter before we turn in?"

Later, we all crawled in under the sticks and lay down on the soft needles. Brewster had to be coaxed to join us because there wasn't much room.

Once we were settled down, I marveled at how wonderful the place smelled, with the children all breathing out peanut butter breath.

They gasped sharply when an awful, ear-splitting shriek pierced the night. Bryan sat up.

"What was that?" he hissed.

"I think it was a fox," my girl said. "I heard one once, and that's what Dad said it was."

"It sounded like someone being *murdered,*" Bryan whispered.

"Nobody's getting murdered, Bryan," Craig told him. "I agree with Maggie Rose. Fox."

"But what if somebody, or some animal, is out there hunting for us?" Bryan replied. His voice was a little unsteady. "We're searching for bears, right? What if that was a bear killing somebody?"

"Well, in that case," Craig said, "I guess we should smear you with peanut butter and shove you out of the shelter."

"Yeah? Or maybe we take you—" Bryan began hotly.

"Please?" Maggie Rose jumped in. "You guys were getting along so well. I just . . . I'm thinking about Mom and Dad getting home and finding us *gone*. We went to look for bears, and we just wound up lost."

She seemed sad. I licked her, and her skin tasted like peanut butter.

The boys were quiet for a moment.

"Well, we didn't find the bears," Bryan said. "But we did save that elk calf, remember?"

"Right," Craig agreed. "And we all had water. And Bryan brought enough peanut butter for an army. And you thought to buy dog treats, Maggie Rose. So we could feed the dogs. We're a good team."

"And Craig, you knew how to build a lean-to," Bryan added.

"Maggie Rose thought of building a dog bed and hugging the dogs," Craig pointed out. "I'm proud of all of us."

"Yeah. Hugging Brewster, I'm almost hot," Bryan said.

At his name, I looked at Brewster. I almost couldn't make out his shape in the gloom, but I could see enough of his face to know he was so, so happy to be sleeping with a boy on each side of him. And my girl had her arms around me.

What a wonderful, wonderful night.

I woke up a short time later. Faintly, very faintly, dancing on the air, I could hear voices far, far away. They were calling names that I recognized.

"Maggie Rose!"

"Craig! Bryan!"

One even called, "Lily!"

I wagged, but I knew I should not leave my girl, not even with someone yelling my name. I could tell they were some distance away, anyway, and I never went far from Maggie Rose if I could help it.

After a while, the voices stopped calling. Silence came back to the night. Brewster sighed, and I closed my eyes, wondering who the people had been.

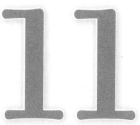

11

I woke up much later, panting. The almost-doghouse in which we were sleeping had become very warm. I glanced at Maggie Rose and saw that she had rolled away from me, snoozing peacefully.

Lying there, I realized what had awakened me. I needed to pee.

I wiggled out from under Maggie Rose's arm and made my way out of our den.

After squatting in the dirt, I lifted my

nose to the night air. The voices had faded away, as had many daytime smells, such as the tang of pine trees in the sun. But a new odor was drifting toward me, one that I recognized because I had learned about it not long ago.

When the large, napping creature had arrived on a rolling bed at Work, I had been surprised by its smell. What animal needs such a strong odor?

The same smell was coming to my nose now.

I wondered if there was a large, snoozing animal lying on a bed with wheels somewhere in the woods, waiting for a person to push it for a car ride. Curious, I let the scent draw me deeper into the forest. The sun was just beginning to brighten the sky.

Soon, I saw I had not tracked a big creature on a bed. Instead, I'd stumbled upon two smaller furry animals, each one about my size.

They were sitting at the base of a big tree, and both turned their heads to stare at me. They had big dark eyes, and noses kind of like a dog's, and round ears that stood up on their heads.

They both darted up the tree, fast as any squirrel, stopping just below the branches to peer down at me.

I was disappointed. Clearly, they had been watching squirrels, and had learned how to climb up a tree instead of how to play.

Were they afraid of me? I was a dog, and yes, I liked chasing squirrels. But I was also happy and playful, and I did not deserve to have them run from me.

I trotted close to the tree and then eased my belly onto the ground. This is how dogs let others know we mean no harm.

The furry animals stared down at me. I wagged and crawled forward on my stomach a little. One of them opened its mouth and squawked at me, a harsh, bawling sound.

I decided not to bark back. Instead, I rolled over onto my back and waved my legs in the air, showing them that I just wanted to play.

Squawker let loose with another unhelpful screech. The other one, his brother, blinked at me.

It was the silent brother who, with a scratching noise, climbed down the tree and dropped to all fours on the ground. I waited patiently while Brother hesitated. I could see that he felt safe next to the tree and didn't want to go away from it. But of course, he was curious about something as remarkable as a dog. He wanted to find out more.

Most animals, except squirrels and a few cats, understand that there is nothing more wonderful than a dog.

I didn't move while Brother sniffed me up and down. When his snout touched mine, I sniffed back. His breath told me he was more hungry than afraid—very hungry. Where were the people who were supposed to feed these two brothers?

When Squawker joined Brother, I very carefully rolled over onto my feet. Wagging hard, I bowed, inviting them to play.

The brothers didn't react at first. This must be what happens to animals who hang out with squirrels too often. They don't get what playing is all about.

Finally, though, Brother put a front paw on my shoulder and pushed a little bit. And we started to play!

These smelly, furry creatures wrestled like dogs! They didn't know that it was rude to spend so much time up on their back legs, but other than that, I could have been playing with Brewster. In fact, they were even more fun than Brewster, because they didn't break away after a short while to collapse into a nap.

They were both very interested in climbing on me, because I was such a fun dog.

When I grew tired of wrestling, I tried Run-with-a-Stick, but they didn't understand that one at all. They were tired, too—tired in that way where being really hungry takes away all your energy.

We plopped down in a heap. They both snuggled up to me, and I realized they were lonely. Where was their mother?

I lifted up my nose and sniffed. Their mother would smell like Brother and Squawker, so that's what I searched for on the air. But there was no sign of her.

I was starting to get worried. What should I do with two young, hungry creatures who needed a mother?

The answer was clear. I should take them back to our new den, the almost-doghouse. There was peanut butter there. Maggie Rose could help find a mother for Squawker and Brother.

I stood up and shook myself and began moving toward where my girl and her brothers were sleeping. But my two new friends didn't understand. They just lay there and watched me.

I did not know what else to do. These were baby animals, and Maggie Rose would want me to take care of them, but they didn't know that they needed to follow me.

"Li-i-i-ly!" I heard a voice cry.

It was Maggie Rose!

I gave up on my new friends and scampered toward the call.

Behind me, Squawker let out a loud, sad squall. It reminded me of the way my littermates and I used to squeal for our mother whenever she left our sides. It meant she should come back to her puppies.

I hoped Squawker's mother would hear him and return to her babies soon.

12

Maggie Rose and her brothers were standing in the chill morning air outside the almost-doghouse. My girl had her hands on her hips. "Lily! Where were you?" she demanded. Brewster glared at me as if I had been a bad dog.

The only way to fix this situation was with love. I went straight to Maggie Rose and jumped up to put my paws on her chest and kiss her face. She still tasted like peanut butter!

"Lily, *no*," she said, pushing me away. "You *stink*!"

"Yeah, she smells horrible," Craig agreed. "She must have rolled in something dead."

Maggie Rose bent over, her nose in my fur. "No!" she exclaimed. "Smell her!"

"I *am* smelling her," Bryan said. "She smells worse than Craig."

"Smell her," my girl insisted.

Reluctantly, Craig shoved his nose at me. I wagged, feeling forgiven. "What is it?" he asked.

"It's bear," Maggie Rose said. "Remember how stinky Dad was? It was this same smell. He said some bears have a strong odor."

They stood up straight and stared at one another. "Lily must have found the cubs!" my girl finally exclaimed. "How else could she smell like this?" She turned to me, snapping my leash into my collar. "Okay, Lily!" she sang. "Take us to the bears!"

I tensed. Clearly, she wanted me to do something. I wondered what it was.

She waved a hand at the trees. I turned, expecting to see squirrels. No squirrels.

"Please, Lily!" my girl pleaded.

"It's just after sunrise," Craig said. "That's when predators are most active. The cubs could be in danger. We need to find them now."

"I thought we were going to eat first," Bryan grumbled.

"Come on, Lily!" my girl told me.

All three humans were very worked up. And it seemed to have something to do with me. So I did Sit, then Lie Down, and then Roll Over. These are my best tricks.

"Oh, Lily," my girl groaned.

"I have an idea," Bryan said. "Brewster!"

The other dog seemed surprised to have everybody's attention. Bryan seized Brewster's head with both hands and guided it to my fur. Brewster sniffed.

"Okay, Brewster. Find the bears!" Bryan exclaimed.

Everyone looked eagerly at Brewster, so I did, too. He gazed back at me, wondering if I understood what we were doing.

Bryan grabbed Brewster's head again and gently lowered Brewster's snout to the ground, guiding him back along the way I'd just come. "Brewster?" he whispered. "Can you find the bears?"

Brewster sniffed the dirt and the pine needles. Then he looked up at me, his nose quivering. He put his muzzle back to the ground and inhaled with a loud *chuff*. Then he took a few steps toward the woods. Bryan followed, keeping the leash slack. "Yes!" Bryan cried out. "Good dog, Brewster!"

Everyone became very excited and we headed into the trees. Soon I realized that we were just walking along the ground I had already covered. So why did all three kids keep saying "Good dog, Brewster"? They were missing the point. *I* was the dog who was good.

We headed down a long slope, and the strong odor of Brother and Squawker filled the air. I saw the instant Brewster figured it out, because his muzzle lifted up from the ground.

I tried to pull on my leash and get ahead of Brewster so that people would understand that I already knew Brother and Squawker, but my girl held me back.

Up ahead, I spotted my two new friends. They bolted for the tree and were up it like squirrels.

"It's them!" my girl said.

"Hey, good dog," Bryan praised. "You did it! You followed the trail, just like I knew you could. You really are a hound dog!" He reached into his pack and Brewster sat and Bryan scooped up a big glob of peanut butter on his fingers. Brewster lapped it up.

I stared in astonishment. What about peanut butter for me?

"Well, give some to Lily, too," Maggie Rose said. "She found them in the first place."

I was grateful when Bryan put his hand

back into his backpack and brought it out with wonderful peanut butter dripping from his fingers. I licked carefully at it until it was all gone.

Brother gazed down at us while Squawker let out one of his loud, screeching calls. Maggie Rose and her brothers stared up at them.

"It's been what, since yesterday, when they could have eaten," Craig muttered. "I'll bet they're starving."

"*I'm* starving," Bryan said.

"I know!" Maggie Rose exclaimed. "I'll bet they'll come down for peanut butter!"

Maggie Rose and her brother looked at Bryan. His eyes widened. "What, are you kidding? We barely have more than two jars left."

"Come on, Bryan. You can have what's left of the third one," Craig replied. "We should give the other two to the bears."

"Yeah, well, we're going to be awfully

hungry when it gets to be night again," Bryan told him.

Craig shook his head. "That's not going to happen. Mom and Dad and probably the entire town of Golden are going to be up here looking for us. Maybe already doing that. We just have to wait for a little while."

"With us here on the ground, the bears are protected," Maggie Rose added. "Especially if they go back up the tree after they've eaten our peanut butter."

"*My* peanut butter," Bryan said.

"Right," Craig told him. "*Your* peanut butter. You are the hero of peanut butter. And your dog tracked Lily's scent back here. We're going to build *you* an airport!"

Bryan sighed. Then he handed my girl two jars from his pack. Brewster and I wagged. Things were looking good!

Except they weren't. Maggie Rose unscrewed both jars of peanut butter and set them at the base of the tree where Squawker was still squalling. I waited with Craig holding my leash, expecting that at any moment he would let me go.

Would Bryan let Brewster have any peanut butter? I hoped so, but it was one of those choices that humans, not dogs, get to make. I would accept it if the peanut butter were all for me.

We backed away from the tree and from the peanut butter, which made no sense. Then we all sat in the dirt.

What could we possibly be doing?

"I hope they come down," my girl whispered.

13

After a long, long wait, Squawker and Brother climbed out of the tree, their claws scratching at the bark. I guess they wanted to show us that they did not know how to eat peanut butter the right way.

Every dog knows that if you're lucky enough to get your teeth on a jar of peanut butter, you have to stick your nose into the opening and scoot the jar around the floor while you lick as hard as you can.

My furry, stinky friends each grabbed a jar in their paws and rolled onto their backs. They held the peanut butter up to their faces and licked.

Brewster and I exchanged disgusted glances.

A wind rose up and ruffled the tree branches. It brought voices to my ears—the same voices I'd heard last night. They were calling names that I recognized.

"Maggie Rose!"

"Bryan!"

"Craig!"

It was Mom and Dad!

I glanced at Brewster and saw that he'd heard, too. He was staring in the same direction as I was.

Then we both looked up at the humans to see how they would react. But they didn't. Apparently watching two stinky fur balls eat peanut butter with their feet was more

important than calling back to Mom and
Dad.

Squawker and Brother were eating food
that was really mine (and maybe a little bit
Brewster's, too). Mom and Dad were yelling
loudly. And I was hungry. All of those things
were starting to make me frustrated.

So I did what any dog would do under the circumstances. I barked.

Brewster must have been frustrated, too, because he barked as well.

Both of my new friends dropped the jars and darted to the tree, heading back up. Maggie Rose and Bryan looked around. Craig peered in the direction Brewster and I were looking.

"Hey! Stop barking," Bryan told us. I wasn't sure what he meant. But since there was peanut butter involved, Brewster and I both decided to be as good as we could be. We stopped barking.

"What do they see?" Maggie Rose asked.

"I don't know," Craig answered.

"Listen!" Bryan said.

The humans fell silent. Brewster did Sit, so I did the same.

The voices came again, closer now, but still faint. "Li-i-ly! Brew-w-wster!"

"That sounded like Dad!" my girl said excitedly. "They heard the dogs!"

The children breathed in at the same time and combined their voices. "Dad!"

Mom and Dad seemed very happy to see me and also their children. We all came together in a hug, even Brewster.

"Is everything okay? Are you all right?" Dad asked.

"We built a lean-to, and we had water and peanut butter," Bryan told him.

"But why did you disobey?" Mom wanted to know. Her face looked stern. "You were told to *stay on the trail around the lake*. Craig?"

"Sorry," Craig mumbled.

"There was a baby elk, and coyotes—" Maggie Rose began.

"You need to understand we've been searching all night," Dad added.

"Craig's phone ran out of battery," Bryan said.

Mom shook her head. "That's not the point. You were not to leave the trail."

Everyone seemed sad, and Mom and Dad were angry. I pressed my side against my girl's legs to give her comfort.

"We've had to send people to look for you who could have been searching for the bear cubs," Dad told the kids.

"So . . . would it help if we found the bears?" my girl asked in a small voice.

Everyone went quiet for a moment. Brewster yawned—he'd gone just about as long as he could without a nap.

"You did?" Dad finally said.

"Yes, sir," Bryan replied. "Lily found them, and then Brewster tracked back to where they were hiding. We gave them peanut butter."

"Where are they?" Mom asked.

The children turned and pointed up into the tree, where Squawker and Brother were gazing down silently. They were probably thinking about climbing back down and finishing off what was left of my peanut butter.

"Well, what do you know?" Dad said, smiling.

We left that place even though there were open peanut butter jars lying on the ground. I could hardly sleep on the car ride Home, I was so upset. But Brewster didn't have any problem snoozing.

I saw Squawker and Brother one more time after that day. It was at a place called "Zoo," where I go with Mom and Maggie Rose sometimes. There are many amazing animal smells at Zoo, but while I am there I am kept on a tight leash and not allowed to explore.

I even have friends at Zoo—Nala and Jax. Nala is a kitten who has grown to be bigger than I am, and Jax is a dog who lives with her. Sometimes the whole reason I am taken to Zoo is to play with the two of them, but not today.

"Is the mother bear all better?" Maggie Rose asked Mom on our car ride.

"I removed the bandages this morning, and she's all healed," Mom answered.

"She'll be really happy to see her babies!" My girl seemed excited, so I licked her hand.

We got to Zoo and headed down the twisting sidewalks. I started to realize we were getting close to some creatures I had smelled before.

My girl was bouncing a little on her toes when we stopped at a high glass wall. In a yard on the other side of the glass, I saw the huge animal I had last smelled when it was sleeping on a rolling bed. It was shuffling along, nose lowered. Then suddenly it stopped and whirled, standing up on its rear legs like a person.

I heard two voices squawking. A cage door rattled and Squawker and Brother ran to the big creature, who lowered down and gathered them up in huge arms. It was like when everyone, even Brewster, joins in a big hug.

Maggie Rose knelt and threw her arms around me. "You did it, Lily. You found the bears, and now they're back with their mommy!"

I licked my girl on the face, happy she was happy.

Her skin still tasted a little like peanut butter.

MORE ABOUT BEARS

There are three kinds of bears in North America: black bears, grizzly bears, and polar bears. Squawker, Brother, and their mother are black bears.

Black bears are the smallest and most common of the three North American bears.

Black bears are not always black. They may be black, brown, reddish, blond, or gray. A few are even white.

A male bear is called a boar. A female is a sow, and the young are called cubs.

Black bears chuff or growl to warn off an intruder. Cubs squall or squeal for their mother if they are frightened. They sometimes make a humming noise a bit like a motor when they are happy.

Bears hibernate in cold weather. They spend weeks and sometimes months asleep in their dens. They live off the fat that their bodies have made in summer and fall.

Cubs are born while a mother is in her den for the winter. The cubs do not hibernate, but they stay close to their mother, drink her milk, sleep, and grow.

Black bear cubs weigh around eight ounces when they are born. That's about the same as two sticks of butter.

Cubs leave the den with their mother when they are around three months old.

Black bears eat mostly grasses, roots,

leaves, and berries. They will sometimes hunt fish and small animals. Unfortunately, many bears learn that garbage cans are good sources of food. This is not healthy for the bears or safe for people. Never feed bears!

FIND OUT HOW IT
ALL BEGAN WITH

A PUPPY TALE

AVAILABLE NOW
FROM STARSCAPE

1

I had a mother and no sisters and too many brothers.

We all lived inside a clean, warm kennel. Our kennel had three walls that I couldn't see through and one that I could. The one I could see through was made of thin wires twisted together. I could glimpse what was on the other side, but I couldn't squeeze through the gaps in the wires.

None of us could, though we tried. We knew there were things out there to smell and taste and chew, more things than we could find inside our kennel home.

Above us was a high ceiling and, in the back of our pen, a soft dog bed. That was where I would sleep with my mother dog, usually with one or more brothers draped across me.

What I saw through the wire, directly across from us, was another kennel just like ours, but empty. I could smell and hear other animals outside our kennels—there were dogs who barked and dogs who didn't and strange-smelling animals who were not dogs and made mewing sounds. Other not-dogs chattered or hissed. But I never saw any of these animals, and they didn't come into the kennel with us.

We had not always lived here. I faintly remembered a different place with different smells. There, I was cold. In the kennel, I was not.

When we lived in the cold place, my only meals had been milk from my mother. Soon after arriving at the kennel, though, I ate different food. The wall that I could see through had a gate that would swing open, and then a woman would come in with soft mush in a bowl.

My mother would greet this woman and lick her hands while her tail wagged happily, so I knew the lady was nice. She was safe. I could trust her. My brothers certainly trusted her; they rushed to her and jumped up toward her face and bit at her hair. I usually hung back so I wouldn't be trampled. But I liked her just the same.

If I didn't have all these brothers, I could have shown

the woman how much I liked her. Also how much I liked her food—which was very much.

But I didn't always get to eat as much of that food as I wanted.

That was because I had too many brothers. I thought about this fact a *lot,* especially when one of them was jumping on me or blocking me from where I wanted to go.

The largest brother was white with gray splotches like me. Another was black with a white tip to his tail, and the third was brown all over. They all had soft ears and big paws and busy tails. So did I. But they were all bigger than I was. A lot bigger, which seemed to lead them to believe they could push me around.

It had always been hard for me to find a place to feed on my mother's milk, because a brother or two would try to shoulder me aside. In the kennel, it was hard for me to gobble up enough meaty mush from the bowl, because my brothers wanted to get there first, and I couldn't always shove my way in.

My brothers stepped on my face when we played. They slept on top of me until I felt flat. They were louder and quicker and rougher than I was, and when we wrestled, I always ended up on the bottom of the pile.

Sometimes I thought life would just be easier without *any* brothers.

If a brother bit my tail or fell down on my head or

stuck a paw in my eye, I yipped or squealed. Then my mother would come to find me. She'd pick me up by the back of my neck. Sometimes, I could feel the gentle bite of my mother's teeth on the nape of my neck before her mouth was even there, feel her warm breath, all in my imagination.

My mother would carry me to the back of our kennel, where our bed was made of soft pillows on the floor. There she'd lie down with me. Her body usually curled into a circle with me at the center.

I loved lying with my mother. She was a girl dog, just like me. I could smell it. We were the only two girls in our kennel. I thought that was why she loved me best.

At least, I hoped she did.

Sometimes, when I was curled up with my mother, I watched people walk by our kennel. That was pretty much all there was to see unless I wanted to look at my brothers. Most of the people would stride busily past, going in one direction or another.

But one day, the woman who brought us food stopped at our kennel. I picked up my head with interest, because she had other people with her! Smaller people who moved more quickly and a bit more clumsily than she did.

Young humans. Children.

My nose twitched. I could smell two boys and a girl.

The boys were bigger; the girl was smaller. Just like *my* family!

I glanced over at my brothers. They weren't paying any attention. As usual, they were piled up in a heap by a wall of the kennel. Brown-Brother was chewing on a toy. Biggest-Brother was chewing on Brown-Brother's leg. White-Tail-Brother was getting ready to jump on Biggest-Brother's head.

"Oh!" said the girl on the other side of the wire. It was a long, drawn-out sound that had both happiness and longing in it. "Oh, puppies!"

I got up and shook myself and scampered forward to investigate.

The girl knelt down and stuck her fingers through the wire. I sniffed at them. They smelled wonderful. I could pick up the scent of salty sweat and soft skin and dirt and something sticky and sweet. She giggled when I started licking. I wagged at the giggles.

Then all my brothers barreled into me. Before I knew it, I was buried under wagging, panting, yipping puppies.

"Get out of the way, Maggie Rose!" I heard someone say.

I wiggled, backing up. When I pulled my head out of the pile of brothers, I saw that the girl was no longer on her knees by the wire. The boys had pushed her to one side so that they could kneel down and put their own fingers into our kennel and laugh as my siblings licked and nibbled and squealed for attention.

I was pretty sure that the girl was the sister and that the bigger boys were her brothers. I could tell by their scents. The way my littermates smelled like me, she smelled like the two boys. Besides, I knew that pushing and shoving was exactly how brothers behaved.

They all had the same brown hair, but the girl's curled at her shoulders, and the boys both had hair that ended close to their heads. The taller one's hair was neatly pushed to one side, while the younger boy had hair that stuck out all over.

"Move over, Craig!" the younger boy said, poking the larger one with his elbow.

"Don't shove, Bryan!" the bigger one answered, pushing back. His breath had an odor on it that I would soon learn came from peanut butter. It was very attractive. I really wanted to know more about peanut butter.

The girl—Maggie Rose?—looked up at the woman. "Mom? Why is the girl puppy so small?" she asked.

"She's the runt of the litter," the woman, Mom, answered. "It happens, honey. One puppy's born small, and then it's hard for her to get her fair share of food or milk, so she doesn't grow as quickly as the others."

The younger boy looked up from where he was letting White-Tail-Brother chew on his fingers.

"Runt—that's what we need to call you, Maggie Rose," he said with a laugh.

I sat and looked at the girl and the mother, high over my brothers' heads. I could see the girl's shoulders and head droop a little at her brother's words.

"Bryan, that's enough," Mom told him sternly. "Make some room for me." Mom reached over to open the gate in the wire wall.

As soon as the gate swung open, my brothers rushed into the hallway, piling onto the boys, jumping up to lick their faces and bite their hands. Craig and Bryan flopped down on the floor, laughing, and my brothers climbed over them just as they did to our mother when they wanted to play.

I stayed inside the kennel. I would have liked to smell and taste these new people close up and to find out if they had any food anywhere. But I knew about this kind of play. It always ended up with me getting squashed and stepped on.

"Oh, puppy, it's okay," Maggie Rose called softly. She sat down and held out her hands. "You can come. Come and see me."

I liked her voice. I wanted to lick her hands some more. Carefully, I stepped around the wrestling boys and brothers and bounded over to Maggie Rose's lap.

She didn't make any quick movements. She touched me gently. Her hands tasted just as good as before. I stuck my nose into the crease under her chin, where her skin was sweaty and delicious.

She giggled. "That tickles!" she said.

"I'm going to name this one Gunner!" declared Bryan, holding up White-Tail-Brother so that his legs paddled in the air.

"This one's Butch!" said Craig, scratching Biggest-Brother's belly.

"How about Rodeo for the brown one?" Bryan said.

"No way. Zev! His name should be Zev!"

"I'm going to name this one Lily," Maggie Rose said. She put an arm around me, and I curled up into a ball in her lap. It felt as cozy as sleeping with my mother.

"No way," Craig said. "How about . . . Katie?"

"How come I don't get to name a puppy?" the girl, Maggie Rose, complained.

"Because you're a runt!" Bryan hooted.

"I'm not going to ask you again, Bryan," Mom warned. "Maggie Rose, of course you can name that puppy if you want."

"Then I'm naming her Lily," Maggie Rose said.

"Stupid name," Craig muttered.

"Why would anybody name a dog after a flower?" Bryan jeered. "She's not even completely white. Lilies are 100 percent white."

"It's my favorite flower," Maggie Rose replied. Her voice was quiet but stubborn. "I'm naming her Lily."

ABOUT THE AUTHOR

W. BRUCE CAMERON is the #1 *New York Times* bestselling author of *A Dog's Purpose, A Dog's Journey, A Dog's Way Home, A Dog's Promise;* the young reader novels *Bailey's Story, Bella's Story, Cooper's Story, Ellie's Story, Lily's Story, Max's Story, Molly's Story, Shelby's Story, Toby's Story;* and the chapter book series Lily to the Rescue. He lives in California.